To my parents, who encouraged my love of music.

No Smiling on Monday

A Story by Jacqueline M. Washack
Illustrations by Donrique

This book is accompanied by the song

"The Monday Morning Blues"

Listen along at
NoSmilingOnMonday.com

Mrs. Wiggles was a wonderful, welcoming music teacher. Her students loved coming to her class because she was full of surprises.

Every morning music filled the air in the music room that was always full of activity.

Mrs. Wiggles loved her students and sometimes she had fun playing tricks on them to teach lessons about music.

After the trick from Mrs. Wiggles, the students always giggled.

One Monday morning, Mrs. Ketchum's kindergarten class came to the music class to sing, dance and have fun learning all about music.

The boys and girls lined up outside the classroom. They were smiling and excited because they loved music with Mrs. Wiggles.

This Monday morning, Mrs. Wiggles stood at the door and greeted their smiling faces with a stern look.

The students were confused because Mrs. Wiggles always smiled, but today, she did not.

So the boys and girls smiled, hoping to cheer her up.

She said "No smiling on Monday." The students were shocked and surprised. They didn't know what to do. Only Jeremy Johnson raised his hand and asked, "Why can't we smile on Monday?"

With a twinkle in her eye, Mrs. Wiggles repeated more forcefully, "No smiling on Monday." Then, she winked at Jeremy.

The young boy looked confused as the students slowly entered the music room with sad eyes and unhappy faces.

Mrs. Wiggles always began her lessons with a familiar song, but today she sat at her piano and sang for the class a new song, "The Monday Morning Blues."

As the students began to learn this new song, they started to smile. Singing does that. Instantly, Mrs. Wiggles stopped playing and reminded them that they could not smile on Monday.

The lesson continued, but there was
no clapping to the rhythm of the new song. No one
played the drums and no one danced to the new
beat because there was no smiling this Monday.
This made the girls and boys sad.

The lesson ended and with sad faces the students left the music room in single file. Jeremy Johnson, who was line leader, was particularly troubled about this new rule.

A week later on Monday, Mrs. Ketchum's kindergarten class once again entered the music room.

Mrs. Wiggles began to review
last week's song,
"The Monday Morning Blues."

The students forgot the new rule and
began to smile as they were singing.

Just then, Jeremy Johnson jumped up, pointed his finger at Mrs. Wiggles and exclaimed, "We have a right to smile on Monday!"

Mrs. Wiggles looked amused and raised her eyebrows. He was puzzled by her expression.

Jeremy continued. "I asked Mrs. Ketchum last week if we could smile on Monday, and she said we could because we had rights as Americans."

Mrs. Wiggles began to laugh. "Of course you can smile on Monday," she said.

The children looked confused.

Mrs. Wiggles was proud of Jeremy for finding out their right to smile on Monday. Mrs. Wiggles said, "I was playing a trick on you because I was teaching you a form of music called the Blues."

Jeremy said, "The Blues? What's the Blues?"

"The Blues is a special kind of song," she explained, "and when you sing the Blues, you feel sad."

"Like on Monday morning, some people feel sad because the weekend is over and it's time to go back to school or work, so they have the blues. But singing makes you happy and soon the blues goes away."

"So let's sing 'The Monday Morning Blues' again."

Mrs. Wiggles' students woefully began singing
"The Monday Morning Blues." Mrs. Ketchum
smiled from the back of the music room as she
listened to her students express themselves
through the song.

And by the time they finished, there were smiles
on all their faces because singing had finally taken
those Monday morning blues away.

The End

As a general music teacher, director of school musicals, and choral director, **Jacqueline Washack** has been working with children on all levels of education from kindergarten through high school. Her passion and humor has instilled a love of music in thousands of students, inspiring many to follow careers in the performing arts.

A humorous incident while teaching a class of smiling kindergarten children on a Monday morning proved the catalyst for No Smiling on Monday. She thanks them for the inspiration.

A Word Of Thanks

I would like to thank all my friends, family, and colleagues for their love and encouragement. A special thanks to cheerleaders, John Cafone, Donna Fazzari, Sharon Fierro, Stafford Horn, Sha Kolcun, Hugh Mahon, Linda Mirabella, Danielle Nice and Megan Washack.

A special thanks to Fran Dubrow and Joe Bravaco for their help with editing and rewrites; to Derek Sammak, for his hard work with this project and his creative and humorous illustrations; to Doris Kempton, my music teacher who inspired me.

To my students, former and present, who have challenged me to become a better teacher. Teaching music has been a realization of a dream.

The Monday Morning Blues

Words and Music:
Jackie Washack

My   eyes are sleep - y and I   want to stay in bed. Our
I'm   here at   last   and it's not so   bad   I said

eyes   are   sleep - y   and   we   want to   stay in bed.   It's
I'm   here at   last   and it's not   so   bad.   The

time   to get a   move on ev - en   though my   eyes are red.   So
teach - ers are all smil - ing ev - en   though they are sad   They're

get out of bed   you lit - tle sleep - y   head.   It's the
fak - ing it too, be -cause it's time for   school They have the

Mon - day morn - ing, Mon - day morn - ing, Mon - day Blues.   I have the
Mon - day morn - ing, Mon - day morn - ing Mon - day Blues.   I have the

Mon - day Morn - ing Blues and I'm not all a - lone.

Peop - le ev' - ry- where are sing - ing the same same song It's the

Mon - day Morn - ing Blues and I'm not all a - lone. So

get out of bed you lit - tle sleep - y head. It's the

Mon - day morn - ing, Mon - day morn - ing, Mon - day Blues. the

Mon - day morn - ing, Mon - day morn - ing, Mon - day Blues. the

School is ov - er and it's time to go home. I said that

school is ov - er and it's time to go home. It

was - n't so bad and I'm not real - ly sad.

I was a fool 'cause school is real - ly cool. Oh the

Mon - day morn - ing, Mon - day morn - ing Blues is gone. Yeah the

Mon - day   Blues   is   gone   ye - ah   the

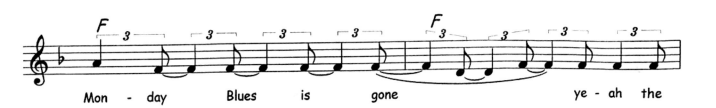

Mon - day   Blues   is   gone   ye - ah   the

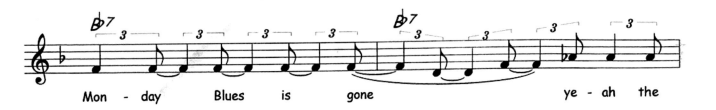

Mon - day   Blues   is   gone   ye - ah   the

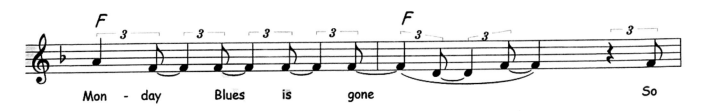

Mon - day   Blues   is   gone   So

get   out   of   bed   you   lit - tle   sleep - y   head.   'Cause   the

Mon - day Morn - ing Blues is   gone,   gone,   yeah!!

The Monday Morning Blues

Verse 1
Mondays are so hard and I have the Blues.
I said that Mondays are so hard and I have the Blues.
The weekend has ended and it's time for school.
So, get out of bed, you little sleepy head.

It's the Monday morning, Monday morning, Monday Blues.

Verse 2
My eyes are sleepy and I want to stay in bed.
Our eyes are sleepy and we want to stay in bed.
It's time to get a move on even though my eyes are red.
So, get out of bed, you little sleepy head.

It's the Monday morning, Monday morning, Monday Blues.

Bridge
I have the Monday Morning Blues and I'm not all alone
People everywhere are singing the same same song.
It's the Monday Morning Blues and I'm not all alone.
So get out of bed you little sleepy head.

It's the Monday morning, Monday morning, Monday Blues.

Verse 3
My backpack is ready and I don't want to go.
I said my backpack is ready and I don't want to go.
My lunch is made oh, I wish it would snow.
It's time to walk to school but I'm moving like a mule.

I have the Monday morning, Monday morning, Monday Blues.

Verse 4

I'm here at last and it's not so bad.
I said I'm here at last and it's not so bad.
The teachers are all smiling even though they are sad.
They're faking it too, because it's time for school.

They have the Monday morning, Monday Morning, Monday Blues.

Bridge

Verse 5

School is over and it's time to go home.
I said that school is over and it's time to go home.
It wasn't so bad, I'm not really sad.
I was a fool because school is really Cool.

Oh the Monday morning, Monday morning Blues is Gone.

Coda

Yeah, the Monday Blues is Gone,
Yeah the Monday Blues is Gone,
Yeah the Monday Blues is Gone.
Yeah the Monday Blues is gone.

So get out of bed you little sleepy head
cause the Monday Morning Blues Gone, Gone, Yeah!

Made in the USA
Lexington, KY
26 June 2018